Stephen Fuller

Notes on the Two Reports from the Committee of the

Honourable House of Assembly of Jamaica

Stephen Fuller

Notes on the Two Reports from the Committee of the Honourable House of Assembly of Jamaica

ISBN/EAN: 9783337330187

Printed in Europe, USA, Canada, Australia, Japan

Cover: Foto ©Andreas Hilbeck / pixelio.de

More available books at **www.hansebooks.com**

N O T E S

ON THE

TWO REPORTS

FROM THE

C O M M I T T E E

OF THE HONOURABLE

House of Assembly of Jamaica, &c.

NOTES

ON THE

TWO REPORTS

FROM THE

COMMITTEE

OF THE HONOURABLE

House of Assembly of Jamaica,

APPOINTED

To examine into, and to report to the HOUSE, the Allegations
and Charges contained in the several Petitions which have been
presented to the BRITISH HOUSE of COMMONS, on the Subject
of the SLAVE TRADE, and the Treatment of the NEGROES,
&c. &c. &c.

BY A

JAMAICA PLANTER.

LONDON:

PRINTED AND SOLD BY JAMES PHILLIPS, GEORGE-
YARD, LOMBARD-STREET.

M.DCC.LXXXIX.

ADVERTISEMENT.

THE following remarks are not publifhed with a view to excite odium againft any individuals, or bodies of men, but to elucidate truth, and to illuftrate this general pofition, that the habitual exercife of that arbitrary dominion which the mafter poffeffes over the flave, communicates an involuntary bias, even to well difpofed minds, againft the juft claims of humanity, and that it is difficult, if not impoffible, to interpofe effectual laws reftraining fuch dominion. Notwithftanding the favourable light in which the framers of the Reports wifh the ftate of the laws in Jamaica previous to the Act of 1788 to be confidered, it is evident from the Reports themfelves, that a very imperfect and limited protection was fecured to the flave. If the flave were killed it was indeed declared to be felony by a law paffed fo lately as 1787, but, the benefit of clergy not being barred, the punifhment, of courfe, was flight, or more properly none at all. As to mutilation, difmemberment, and numberlefs modes of cruelty under which the flave might fuffer, he appears to have been left very much at the difcretion of his mafter:

A   For

For though a penalty of 100l. was laid on the master for such mutilation or dismemberment, yet as the testimony of the slave was not admissible against him, it is not probable that it could ever be recovered; and the 8th clause of the Act of 1781 (Report, p. 6.) which ordains the punishment of fine and imprisonment *on any person wantonly beating a slave not his own property*, plainly denotes the insecurity of the slave from such wanton assaults of his own master. The infrequency too of publick executions (p. 9.) seems to indicate either that the conduct of the slaves was not so vicious as has been represented, or that the master was accustomed to assume to himself the offices of judge, jury, and executioner. What indeed can be thought of the humanity of that code of laws which permitted mutilation and maiming, as judicial punishments for crimes! (see Report, p. 17). Every one who knows how deeply power corrupts the human heart, will lament the humiliating condition of the slaves, when so much licence was allowed to bad tempers, and when the very system of slavery tends to create or inflame such tempers.

The instance of suffering these lenient and salutary laws, *as they are called*, to lie totally extinct for three years, viz. from 1784 to 1787, (Report, p. 6.) is a striking proof of their inefficacy, and of the little regard paid to them.

The last law, passed in Jamaica in 1788 affords, however, a prospect of meliorating the situation of the slaves. A new law in Grenada professes the same benevolent purpose. Laws of melioration and

and improvement are a credit to thofe who promote them, but they certainly imply former defects, and nothing can more fully confirm the accounts which are given of the tyranny of mafters, than this tacit acknowledgment of the little reftraint they were, till lately, under. This, indeed, is exprefsly admitted in the preamble to the Grenada Act, which is as follows:

" Whereas the laws made for the protection of
" flaves have been found *infufficient*, and whereas
" humanity and the intereft of the colony re-
" quire that falutary and adequate regulations
" and provifions fhould be adopted for rendering
" their fervitude as limited and eafy as poffible,
" and for promoting the increafe of their popu-
" lation, as the moft likely means of removing in
" the courfe of time the neceffity of further im-
" portations of negroes from Africa: And where-
" as thefe defirable ends cannot be fo effectually
" obtained, as by prefcribing *reafonable bounds to*
" *the power of mafters and others having the charge*
" *of flaves,* by compelling them fufficiently and
" properly to lodge, feed, clothe, and maintain
" them, by introducing them to the knowledge
" of the Chriftian religion, and affording them
" opportunity of improvement in morality, and by
" inducing them to regular marriage, and when
" married, protecting them in their conjugal rights."
Be it therefore enacted, &c.

After all, when it is confidered that the diftance between a mafter and a flave is infinitely greater than that between any other fituations in human life, it may well be doubted whether any laws can be fo framed as to afford effectual protection to the flave. If it is difficult, even in this free country, for a poor man to obtain legal redrefs for the oppreffion of the rich, how much more difficult muft it be in countries where the dominion of the rich is fo abfolute, that the murmurings of complaint may be refented as an affront, and punifhed as a crime? While ‘ local policy’ ufurps the feat of equity, and ‘ requires a diftinction between the modes of trying black or white perfons,’† the adminiftration of juftice muft be very defective and partial.

If, however, the planters by thefe Acts fincerely mean a gradual improvement in the ftate of the flaves, let us rejoice in the hope that a melioration of the ftate of flavery will be accompanied by a melioration of the tempers of the flave-holders, and that, by degrees, fuch manners and principles will prevail, as will render acts of tyranny and cruelty difgraceful in the eyes of the country. May the fpirit of humanity, and the love of freedom, fo congenial to the Britifh nation, extend their influence till the legiflatures, both national and provincial, may perceive that no fubftantial and durable intereft can be derived from fo polluted a fource as flavery !

THE EDITOR.

† See Report, p. 16 in the notes.

N O T E S

O N   T H E

R E P O R T S.

To ———

IN a former letter I mentioned the two Reports publifhed by our Houfe of Reprefentatives on the applications of the people in Britain to the Houfe of Commons, for the Abolition of the African Slave Trade; and having charged the faid Reports with wilful deception, and holding out of falfe lights, I think it neceffary to prove the charge, which I apprehend will be done by tran-fcribing the pencilled notes I made in the margin of the printed copies of the faid Reports, on the firft curfory perufal thereof. But firft I will pre-mife, that " the Committee, appointed to inquire " into and report to the houfe the Allegations and " Charges, contained in the feveral petitions which " have been prefented to the Britifh Houfe of " Commons on the fubject of the Slave Trade, and " the Treatment of the Negroes, &c. &c. &c." had two objects in view, and for the effecting of which the Reports are calculated, more than with any real intention or hope of folidly refuting the allega-tions and charges contained in the faid petitions,

many

many of which the Committee knew were too well grounded in facts to be refuted.

The first object the Committee had in view was a very laudable one. There had been prepared, and was then pending, a bill for securing more impartial trials and better treatment to slaves; and the Committee were well informed that every opposition would be given to it in the Council. Those who disliked the bill, that is, those who did not like to have any penalties or restrictions laid on that cruelty, and injustice, which they were conscious they had been, and probably intended to be again, guilty of, said confidently, and people generally apprehended, that it would be thrown out by the Council. Some of the more sensible and humane members of the Committee conceived that, by quoting in their Report several of the most favourable clauses of the bill, that is, those which they apprehended would meet with most opposition in the Council, and be more like to occasion the miscarriage of the bill; by reasoning on, and taking credit for those clauses; by sending their report to the Governor, for his transmission of it to the Secretary of State, in order to its being laid before the King in Council; by publishing it, by printing it here, and by directing the Agent of the Island in London, to print it there, and not only to present copies thereof to the Members of each House of Parliament, and to each of the bodies which had petitioned the House of Commons, but also dispersing it generally through the kingdoms, the Legislature would be pledged to pass the bill into a law, and the Council seeing the disreputation and ill consequences that would result from their refusing

to

to give their affent, would alfo pafs it, and it was known that the Governor was with the bill: or on the other hand, fhould the Council after all, determine to reject it, the odium would fall alone on that board, and not on the people at large, or on their reprefentatives, who had fhewn their willingnefs to have the law made, by having originated and paffed it, which would tend to their exculpation in the eyes of the publick from the charges of cruelty and tyranny, more than any thing that could be offered in difproof of the allegations. I am afraid that too many wifhed for this cheap and plaufible mode of exculpation, which would coft them nothing; for if the bill did not pafs into a law, they would have credit for all that was good in it without being bound to the conceffions which conftituted that good: " *How can the people of* " *Britain blame, or the Legiflature go about to* " *punifh, us for abufes which we wifh to reform, but* " *are prevented from reforming by the Board of* " *Council appointed by themfelves ;—fay by the* " *Crown ?*"—With fuch as held up this dangerous idea, I reafoned thus: The ifland ftands pledged by the Report, to pafs the bill into a law, and if it fhall not be paffed, what can the nation think but that there has been a bafe collufion between the two branches of the Legiflature here? Will not they argue after this manner? " Was there ever fo bafe, fo vile a fubterfuge as this? They ftood charged with cruelty, tyranny, and injuftice, and how do they act under the charges?—We confefs, fay they, to the publick of Great Britain, (who are their accufers) we confefs, that the laws refpecting our flaves, are not fo good as they might be; you have called our attention to them, and we fee that they

A 4 require

require amendments; we thank you, and we will forthwith make the requisite amendments; our Assembly are already forward in the salutary work; they have prepared a bill, which when passed into a law, will secure our slaves from cruel treatment, and partial trials. But whilst they in effect say this, by publishing the Reports of their Assembly, nothing is farther from their intentions, than that such bill should be passed into a law. They knew that by a collusive agreement it was to be rejected by their Board of Council — they knew that Parliament would meet early, and that the House of Commons was pledged to take cognizance of the petitions on the Slave Trade amongst the first objects of their attention; and they conceived that the two Reports of their Assembly, and the copy of the bill alluded to, would not only satisfy the House, but also appease the petitioners at large, and the business would be suffered to die away; and they flattered themselves, that as the bill, by concert, would not finally be rejected till the close of their Session, before an account of its rejection could reach to Britain, it would be too late in the session here to resume a business of such importance, as the Abolition of the African Slave Trade. Surely those people are hardened in iniquity, and lost to all sense of shame." May not the people in Britain, I said, reason in this manner, and in resentment of such unworthy conduct, may not their indignation lead them to acts of severity, which they would not otherwise have thought eligible? And what but the detestation of all good men can be expected from such vile duplicity as we shall be thought guilty of? Do you suppose, that the people of Britain will easily lose sight of this great national business, in which

which they are now involved ? For after the matter hath been brought into open light, and agitated fo, that no man can plead ignorance on the fubject, it now concerns them as a nation; if they wink at our crimes, they will be partakers of our guilt, and muft expect to partake of our punifhment. I am perfuaded, that there are myriads of men of fober minds, and cultivated underftandings, as well as tender confciences, who think thus, for all who believe " that there is a God that judgeth the " earth," muft think fo, and therefore they will not, they cannot with peace, lofe fight of it. But fome may fay, Do you efteem it no injury to lofe a whole day's labour of our flaves out of every twelve ? And is it nothing that negroes and flaves fhall be tried like white men, like free Britifh men, by grand and petit juries ?—What poffible injury can that do to white men, if thofe juries, who are themfelves white men, do juftice on fuch trials ? —But they are not by the bill to be tried like Britifh men—*they are not to be tried by their Peers.*— But, are the eternal rules of juftice to bend to the pride and caprice of one fet of men, who happen, by fome means, to be poffeffed with " *a little brief* " *authority,*" to the prejudice and mifery of others ? Do you really fuppofe, that there are two forts of juftice with that Being who made all men of one flefh, though not all of one colour, and who is no refpecter of perfons, but amongft all nations and people, accepts of them who do juftly, love mercy, and fear to offend him ? As to this day in two weeks, I am convinced, on good grounds, that it would not be loft; it would be a benefit to all who chearfully granted it. Does not the experience of all ages and nations fhew, that in every climate, and

most

moſt in hot and debilitating ones, ſuch as this, reſt after labour is neceſſary? The Being, who created man, who knows his frame, and what his nature requires, has declared, that one day's reſt after ſix of labour is requiſite. Juſtice and obedience to the moral law out of the queſtion, and conſidering negroes merely as labouring animals, will not their ſtrength be renewed and invigorated by returns of reſt, and will not they be thereby enabled to do more work in five days, ſo recruited, than in ſix, exhauſted and diſpirited by continual toil?—But that they would is not a matter of conjecture, or of argument: I have the irrefragable teſtimony of experience for it that they will. I give, I beg pardon, reaſon and humanity *give*, and I *allow*, them one day in each week to labour for themſelves; God has given them another of reſt from their labours; and I find, that in the other five they do more work without whipping, or fear of whipping, than many other peoples do in ſix, though urged by cruel ſeverity.—Count what is loſt by unwillingneſs and deſertion, by advertiſing runaways, and ſending out parties to ſearch for and bring them in, and ſee to what it amounts? I have no deductions of that kind to make, for I have not, for years paſt, had one negroe abſent for a day, without leave, though I take not the cruel, though common precautions to prevent their running away, by branding their fleſh with the letters of my name, or the marks of my plantations.—It is to be hoped I brought over ſome to my way of thinking.—But to come back to the other object aimed at by the Committee in their Reports: It was ſimply to exculpate the iſland from the charges of cruelty, injuſtice, and tyranny; at any rate, right or wrong, to exculpate us.

This

This is a heavy charge, but I will prove it, and challenge any man of honour to deny it. Two of the moſt active Members in the Committee, both men of great humanity, whoſe negroes are treated with uncommon lenity, were earneſt to purge the iſland from the charges of cruelty and injuſtice, which they thought did not exiſt, and they ſet about collecting ſuch proofs and vouchers as they conceived would teſtify to the world how much the people of this iſland were miſrepreſented, and how injuriouſly calumniated; but what was their aſtoniſhment, when the inquiry which they had inſtituted, and from which they expected to refute the allegations and charges contained in the petitions to the Houſe of Commons, furniſhed the moſt indiſputable teſtimonies that the charges of cruelty, tyranny, and injuſtice were well founded? Cruelty and tyranny in the treatment of negroes by individuals, and publick partiality and injuſtice in trials, both of white people for ſuch cruelty, and of negroes for crimes of which they ſtood charged.— What was to be done then? " If we report generally that ſome of the allegations and charges may be true, there will be great danger; but if we report particularly the reſult of our inquiries, there *will be an abſolute certainty of the Slave Trade being aboliſhed.* Let us then throw a veil over the paſt, ſince we can neither recall nor juſtify it; but let us exert ourſelves, by all means, to prevent the like enormities in future."

I come now to my notes on the two Reports of the Houſe, which were written as I read them: they will tend to give a juſter idea of the ſubject, perhaps, than a more elaborate treatiſe.

NOTES

NOTES ON THE FIRST REPORT.

" P. 2. The Committee are of opinion, that the
" principle of the faid Act of the Britifh Parliament*
" is founded in juftice, humanity, and neceffity;
" and that the provifions adopted therein, when
" further matured by the wifdom of parliament,
" muft ultimately prove highly beneficial to the
" fugar colonies, inafmuch as it is notorious, that
" veffels have been frequently crowded with a
" greater number of negroes than they ought in
" prudence to have contained. And it is the opi-
" nion of the Committee, that the wifdom and
" authority of parliament might be beneficially
" exerted, in further regulations of the African
" commerce; particularly, in preventing the de-
" tention of fhips on the coaft ; in prohibiting the
" purchafe of flaves who fhall appear to have been
" kidnapped, or deprived of liberty contrary to
" the ufage and cuftom of Africa; and in com-
" pelling the faid fhips to tranfport an equal num-
" ber of both fexes, and to provide ventilators,
" and a fufficient quantity of provifions, efpecially
" water.——It feems not to be underftood in
" Great Britain, that the inhabitants of the Weft
" India iflands have no concern in the fhips trad-
" ing to Africa:—The African trade is purely a
" Britifh trade, carried on by Britifh fubjects re-
" fiding in Great Britain, on capitals of their own;
" —the connexion and intercourfe between the
" planters of this ifland, and the merchants of
" Great Britain trading to Africa, extend no fur-
" ther than the mere purchafe of what Britifh acts
" have declared to be legal objects of purchafe."

* The Act paffed laft feffion.

With

With refpect to the crowding of veffels, fee notes in the fequel, on the examination of Meffrs. Chifolme, Anderfon, and Quier.

The tender care profeffed here by a Jamaica Houfe of Affembly, for the rights and liberties of the natives of Africa, is too extraordinary a circumftance not to ftrike the obfervation of the reader. Thofe who have given any attention to the publications on the ufe, propriety, and juftice, of the flave trade, will have obferved that of thofe who defend the benefit, right and juftice, the moft able, that is, the moft artful, perceiving the impoffibility of juftifying our making flaves, or the encouraging others in the making flaves, of thofe who are born in a ftate of natural and political freedom, either deny that the natives of Africa have fuch rights, or allege that they have forfeited them to the laws of their country by crimes, the punifhment of which is flavery. Some defcribe the governments in Africa to be univerfally pure defpotifm, or they argue as if they fuppofed they were fuch, and conclude that the ftate of flavery in the Britifh colonies is fo much preferable to the condition our flaves were removed from, that the change is a real bleffing. Long, on this fubject, (fee chapters, I. II. III. Book 3. of the 2d vol. of his Hiftory of Jamaica, intitled Negroes) determined to lay a folid foundation for the wicked conclufions he intended to draw, fuppofes them fcarcely, if at all, fuperior to brute beafts; the conclufion from which is, that they were meant for the flaves of men, white men to be fure, or Indians; for, according to Mr. Long, negroes are hardly
men,

men. Then having reasoned them down to a level with ourang outangs, or rather the ourangs up to, or rather above the negroes, he proceeds to state that their government is so arbitrary, and their condition so absolutely slavish, that it is a great melioration of their state to transfer them to the condition of slavery, them and their posterity, in Jamaica or the other islands. *Now* we see it is admitted that there are free people in Africa, and an anxious care is taken by the legislature of Jamaica to observe that the rights of those free men shall not be infringed, lest it might draw the good people of Jamaica into the dreadful predicament of having bought as slaves those who had a right to freedom. Now, if one who has seen how negroes are sold on board a Guinea ship were to read this passage, and were to ask those conscientious committee men this question :—" You see, " Gentlemen, how very necessary it is to guard " against the kidnapping of free people of Africa, " and until some care shall be taken in that par- " ticular by the wisdom and authority of the " British parliament, pray how do you intend to " guard yourself from partaking in the same guilt " as the kidnapper ? How have you guarded against " it hitherto ? I suppose you either took with you a " linguist, and examined those you intended to buy " some days before the sale; or if that could not be, " and as it is impossible at the sale, then I suppose " on taking them home you went through the ne- " cessary scrutiny, and on finding that the negro was " born free, and had not forfeited that freedom by " committing felony, of course you restored him to " that liberty of which he was unjustly deprived."

I say,

I fay, was any man ferioufly to put this queftion to the very men who framed that claufe, they would laugh in his face. Let me fpeak out, that claufe and feveral others in the bill, are merely held out to amufe the people at large in England, but here has no meaning, and I quote it to fhew the low artifices which even a legiflative body are obliged to ftoop to, when to fupprefs what is true, and to affect what has no exiftence, becomes neceffary to fupport the caufe they advocate.

The falutary effects of ventilators in fhips navigating tropical climates when crowded with people, is too well known to need any farther argument. I will only obferve on this paffage, that if government fhall not think proper immediately to abolifh the flave trade, but in humane confideration of the horrible condition of negroes in Guinea fhips, fhall by law oblige the owners of thofe fhips to provide them with ventilators; that care be taken that they be conftructed fo as to perform their office by the agency of fire, wind, or the motion of the fhip through the water, or by all of them; and not to require the labour of men to work them: and that proof fhall be made on the entry of the fhips in the iflands, that fuch ventilators have been kept conftantly operating: otherwife fome things to which the names of ventilators may be given, will be put up merely to avoid the penalty of the law, but without anfwering the good purpofe intended.

"P. 3. The Committee are further of opinion, that " as to the charges and allegations brought againft " us, with regard to the treatment and fituation

" of

" of flaves in this ifland, it is neceffary, and eafy,
" to difprove the fame, by demonftrating, 1ft, that
" negroes in this ifland are under the protection
" of lenient and falutary laws, fuited to their fitu-
" ation and circumftances;—2dly, that the flave-
" laws are executed with humanity, mildnefs, and
" mercy;—3dly, that the laws have made pro-
" vifions to grant flaves days of reft, and to prevent
" their being in want of the neceffaries of life;—
" and, 4thly, that the decreafe of our flaves does
" not arife from the caufes alledged in the peti-
" tions prefented to the Britifh Houfe of Com-
" mons, but from various other caufes not im-
" putable to us, and which the people in Great
" Britain do not feem to comprehend."

For Remarks on the lenity of thefe laws, and of
their execution, vide Notes on the Second Report.

SECOND

SECOND REPORT.

For Obfervations on the renewal of the act of 1784, fee note farther on.

" On this fubject we have to obferve, that it
" appears by the letters of our Agent, that cer-
" tain heads of inquiry were tranfmitted to him
" a few months ago, from a Committee of the
" Lords of His Majefty's Moft Honourable
" Privy Council, many of which related to
" the condition and government of our flaves;
" and, in anfwer thereto, an abftract of moft of
" our ancient flave-laws were laid before their
" Lordfhips; to which, if neceffary, reference may
" be had; but it feems not to have been under-
" ftood by our Agent, that in 1781, many of thofe
" laws were repealed, and all the fubfifting laws
" and claufes of laws refpecting the order and go-
" vernment of flaves were confolidated and brought
" into one act:—This act is known by the name
" of the Confolidated Slave Act; and, having ex-
" pired on the 31ft day of December 1784, has
" fince been renewed, with amendments. By
" the faid act of 1781, Claufes 2d and 3d, all pof-
" feffors of plantations are obliged, under the pe-
" nalty of 50l. to allot provifion grounds for each
" of their flaves, to allow them fufficient time to
" work the fame, and alfo to keep in proper cul-
" tivation one acre of land, at leaft, for every four
" negroes in plantain-walk and ground-provifions,
" exclufive of the negroes grounds; and in cafe
" the owners or poffeffors have not lands proper
" for that purpofe, they are required to make

B   " fome

" fome other ample provifion for the fupport of
" their flaves."

With refpect to allowing *fufficient* time to work,
as no time was fpecified by the act as *fufficient*, nor
any made compulfory, none was allowed; and
therefore this claufe, though plaufible, and quoted
here as a proof of lenity, never operated in favour
of one negro in the ifland, fo far as to procure him
the allowance of one hour, which the framers of
the Report knew well, and which they own, when
they come to claim credit for the parallel claufe in
the new bill. And I think it is no breach of
charity to affert, that when the claufe was inferted
in the law, it was forefeen that as it was not compulfory on any, none would obey.

" By claufe 4th it is enacted, that every mafter,
" owner, or poffeffor of flaves fhall, under the fame
" penalty, provide and give to each flave proper
" and fufficient cloathing, to be approved of by
" the juftices and veftry of the parifh."

As the act did not fpecify what quantity of
cloathing was to be deemed *fufficient*, nor compel
the juftices and veftry to take cognizance of the
fubject, they of courfe did not take any. This
claufe therefore, like the preceding one, was fpecious, but nugatory, I fhall in a fubfequent note
affign the real motives of thefe and fimilar non-
effective claufes being inferted.

" By claufe 5th, flaves giving information of
" thefts, or other crimes and mifdemeanors, are en-
" titled to pecuniary rewards; which is one proof,
" among

" among others, that our laws confider flaves as
" capable of holding property, and will protect
" them therein."

Why did not the Committee when they were
exprefsly employed in quoting laws and claufes of
the humane, mild, and falutary laws, why, I fay,
did not they quote the law, or claufes of laws, by
which negroes are protected in the poffeffion of
property? Is it the law that orders them to be
whipped for having more than five pound of meat
in their poffeffion?

" By Claufe 6th, the penalty of £. 100. is laid
" on any mafter or owner who fhall mutilate or
" difmember any flave or flaves."

To people in Britain it muft appear ftrange, firft,
that there fhould be a neceffity for a law to punifh
mafters for mutilating and difmembering their fervants; and ftill ftranger, that a law fhould be ex-
tant for inflicting fuch punifhment from the year
1717, and that great numbers of inftances fhould
be notorioufly known to magiftrates and judges, as
well as others, of people having mutilated their
negroes without any perfon whatever recollecting,
at the times when fuch inftances made it neceffary to
put the law in force, that there was fuch a law;
ftranger ftill, that the Committee fhould gravely
affect aftonifhment at the people of England,
alleging fuch things, when a little inquiry
would have convinced them — of what? that
the allegations *were totally groundlefs?* — no, by
no means. But fuch inquiry would have convinced
them that the minds of men become indurated by

B 2   the

the habitual profpect of oppreffion and mifery. Hundreds of inftances, aye doubtlefs thoufands, of difmemberments, mutilations, and abfolute murders have occurred, which, by reafon of the evidence of negroes not being competent againft white men, cannot be cognizable by magiftrates. I know two men, now living, whofe neighbours fay pofitively, and every body believes, that each of them has murdered fcores of their own negroes. One of thofe monfters has been heard to fay, that fince he became a planter on his own account, which was rather late in life, he had buried, as he termed it, 357 negroes : and yet this execrable being, affected to be aftonifhed at a perfon's being fo unpolite as to tell him, that if what his neighbours faid of him was true, the wonder was not that he had buried fo many, but that he had any above ground.

I muft not, however, omit to give the claufe of amendment in the law of 1787 the praife it juftly merits; it is a good claufe, and not at all to be blamed for its not having been put in force oftner than it has been. I have for many years been converfant with Jamaica, and know but of one inftance of the law againft mutilation being inforced, and that inftance occurred fince the people in Britain have interefted themfelves in favour of the poor negroes : I have been fpeaking of the Act of 1717, but there is an amendment in the Act of 1787, which will have a good effect.

" By Claufe 7th it is enacted, that in cafe any per-
" fon fhall mutilate any flave the property of ano-
" ther, fuch further punifhment would be in-
" flicted, exclufive of the aforefaid fine, as the
" Court

" Court fhould think proper; and at the fame time
" the owner of the injured flave is allowed to pur-
" fue his remedy for damages at common law."

The *owner* of the injured flave is allowed to
purfue, &c. And in the name of juftice and
mercy, why not the *injured flave* alfo allowed? Is
this difallowance amongft the other proofs that the
law will protect him in the poffeffion of property,
when it provides no remuneration for the lofs of
his limbs or members? Why, if the criminal is
poffeffed of property, ought not he to be compelled
to make reftitution to the *injured flave* by pur-
chafing his liberty, and providing for his fupport?

" By Claufe 8th, any perfon wantonly beating
" a flave, not his own property, is liable to be
" indicted for the fame, and punifhed by fine and
" imprifonment."

The preceding note applies equally to this claufe,
why fhould the immediately injured be precluded
all redrefs—in this world?

" When we reflect that many of thefe claufes were
" provifions of our ancient laws; and, in parti-
" cular, that the penalty on the mafter who fhould
" mutilate or difmember his flave, was enacted fo
" long ago as the year 1717; and when we confider
" further, that the faid act of 1781 was in full
" force until 31ft December 1784; we cannot
" fufficiently exprefs our aftonifhment and con-
" cern, that refpectable bodies of men fhould have
" fubfcribed their names to allegations, which a

B 3   " little

" little inquiry muſt have convinced them were
" totally groundleſs,"

" Enacted ſo long ago as 1717," ſince then there
have been numberleſs diſmemberments, publickly
known, which paſſed unnoticed by authority. I
know one extraordinary inſtance of a man, I believe ſtill alive, who diſmembered his only negroe, and now is or lately was led about by that
very negroe; the inhuman maſter having, ſoon after
his barbarity to the poor ſlave, loſt his ſight. This
is a notable anſwer to the argument made uſe of by
ſome who are averſe to reſtraining laws, viz. that a
man's ſlaves being his property, a regard to his own
intereſt will prevent his injuring their life, health,
or ſtrength. I aſked one of thoſe advocates for un-
controlled power, if he ever knew a man hurt his
horſe by over-riding him ? Oh yes. Had he ever
known a man injure his health by drinking or other
exceſs ? Oh yes, many. Had he ever known any
who had by gaming, or other extravagance, ruined
their fortune, and brought their wives and children
to diſtreſs and want ? By this time he diſcovered
what I aimed at, and was ſilent.

We ſee by the next paragraph, that the protection of the limbs and lives of the negroes was of
ſo little weight with the legiſlature here, that they
ſuffered the law of 1784, ſo much vaunted for
affording that protection, to expire, and the
wretched ſlaves to remain at the mercy (that is, the
cruelty) of whoever choſe to abuſe them for three
years.

" By

" By Claufe 4th, regulations are made to prevent
" flaves being deferted in future by their owners,
" on account of age and infirmity; and, by a fub-
" fequent claufe, the juftices and veftry of each
" town and parifh are empowered to lay a tax upon
" the inhabitants, for providing food, medical
" care, and attendance, on flaves already deferted
" by their owners, and who are difabled from
" labour by ficknefs, old age, or otherwife. And,
" in order more effectually to enforce the regula-
" tions of former laws, refpecting the fubfiftence
" and cloathing of flaves, it is enacted, by Claufe
" 6th, That every mafter, owner, or attorney,
" fhall, under a penalty of fifty pounds, give in
" to the veftry, on oath, an account of the quan-
" tity of land in ground provifions (over and
" above the negro grounds), for the ufe of their
" flaves ; or, in cafe there are not lands proper for
" the purpofe, an account on oath of the means
" adopted for the maintenance and fupport of their
" flaves ; and alfo, under the like penalty, give in
" an account of the cloathing actually ferved to
" each flave."

The whole of the claufes mentioned here are excellent. This is not only making laws, but providing for their being executed; but as for " the
regulations of former laws," as they are here
termed, they were not when made, nor till thefe
claufes were created, ever meant to be enforced.
The giving into the veftry an account on oath of
the quantity of land in provifion, and of cloathing
furnifhed to the negroes, will I think have the beft
effects; and the providing for deferted negroes, was
liftening at length to an evil of enormous mag-

nitude,

nitude, which had long cried to heaven for vengeance. Horrible cruelties had been exercised in regard to negroes, who were rendered incapable of labouring by age or sickness, whose execrable masters, after having had the labour of all the healthy and vigorous years of their lives, deserted them in age, sickness, and imbecility; deserted them to all the horrors of nakedness, hunger, and helpless old age. But the guilt ended not there; some of those poor wretches in this situation would steal provisions, or something wherewith to procure provisions; and if detected, the master of the slave so detected, the very master who had deserted him, became his prosecutor; because being convicted and executed, he, the master, became intitled to and received from the publick forty pounds.

On this head let me mention a single circumstance. A planter once on a journey to Kingston, put up for the night at an inn kept by one Bailey, a strange fellow, but who was not destitute of humanity. In the dead of the night the house was alarmed with a cry of thieves. It was then the fashion to travel armed. On the alarm, the planter snatched up his sword, and ran out of the door, where he presently seized on a man who was breaking into the provision store. He had just secured him, with his back to the wall, and the point of his sword to his breast, when the people brought lights, and discovered this dreadful house-breaker to be a tall emaciated old man, whose woolly head was as white as snow, and who seemed hardly able to stand. The negroes immediately mentioned his name to the inn-keeper, who ordered them to bring him in, and gave direction to bring victuals and

drink

drink with as much glee, as if the old man had arrived in a coach and fix. The planter was pleafed at his humanity, as he thought it, but was furprized at his frequently thanking the poor creature for coming to break into his ftore, and charged him always to come when he wanted victuals, and if the people were a fleep to break the pantry or the ftore.—
" You feem furprized, Sir, fays he to the planter, but I will difappoint the fcoundrel." — " What fcoundrel ?"—" This poor fellow's mafter, Sir. I have known this negroe fixteen years, when he was worth any fix negroes his mafter had; faithful, diligent, and fkilful; but now he is worn down by age, and is grown filly, the fcoundrel drives him away, in hopes that he will break into fome houfe to fteal, and be apprehended, when he will become the profecutor, and claim by the law of the ifland forty pounds. But I will circumvent the rafcal." And then he laid the ftricteft injunction on his houfe-keeper, and fervants, always to encourage the old man to come there for food. Now I am fpeaking of cruelty exercifed on an old man, what will be thought of a chief juftice of the ifland, whom I knew well ? This man having heard that a favourite negroe man, in the vigour of his life, belonging to himfelf, was convicted and condemned to be hanged, fent off the fellow, under pretence of having him executed on the property he belonged to, in terrorem, to the other negroes, to a diftant eftate, and had a fuperannuated old watchman, paft labour, hanged up in the ftead of the criminal. It feems that the old man's name was Mingo; and the only punifhment the mafter underwent was that of being denominated in the party writings of that time, which were violent, *Old Mingo.*

By

" By Claufe 9th, the penalty on perfons mutilating
" or difmembering their flaves is increafed, by ad-
" ding to the fine of 100 l. inflicted by former laws,
" the punifhment of imprifonment, not exceed-
" ing twelve months; and, in certain cafes, mu-
" tilated flaves are to be declared free :—and in all
" fuch cafes the Court is authorized to direct, that
" the fine of 100 l. be paid over to the juftices and
" veftry of the parifh, who, in confideration there-
" of, are to allow to fuch flave declared free, ten
" pounds per annum for maintenance and fupport,
" during life. By the fame claufe the juftices and
" veftry are appointed a council of protection, for
" the purpofes of making full inquiry into the
" mutilation of flaves, and for profecuting to effect
" fuch owner or owners as may have been guilty
" thereof. And by Claufe 10th it is enacted, That
" in cafe any information is made before any juftice
" of the peace, that any flave or flaves is or are
" mutilated and confined, it fhall and may be law-
" ful for fuch juftice of the peace, and he is re-
" quired, to iffue his warrant to the marfhal or
" conftable, to bring the flave or flaves before him
" for infpection. By this regulation the power of
" concealment is endeavoured to be taken from the
" owner; for, as it is not required that the in-
" formation fhould be on oath, the magiftrate is
" enabled to obtain a view of the fact, on evidence
" which, in other cafes, is, and ought to be, in-
" admiffible."

The whole matter of thefe claufes, like that of
the preceding one, is moft excellent, and will be
attended with the moft falutary confequences; for
by the words *any information,* certainly the information

mation from a negroe fhould authorize the magiftrate to iffue his warrant, and the knowledge of
this will be the means of preventing cruelty, or
of detecting it.—The application of the fine, li-
berating the negroe, and appointing the juftices
and veftry a Council of protection, are all fraught
with wifdom and juftice, and fhew that the Affembly is in earneft to put a ftop to cruelty. Indeed their
conduct, that is, of a majority of them, refpecting
the bill, is highly praife-worthy; but one cannot help
regretting, that this law, or fomething like it, had
not been paffed long fince. We became poffeffed of
the ifland of Jamaica, I think, in A. D. 1655, and
in 1781, nay, in 1788, that is 133 years after, we
are beginning to make laws, for the firft time effectual laws, for the protection of the lives and limbs
of our negroes ! What bloody entries have been
made in the indelible records of heaven in that
period ?

" By Claufe 11th, it is enacted, That if any
" perfon fhall murder any flave, whether his own
" property or not, he fhall fuffer death for fuch
" offence."

" And, in order more effectually to prevent the
" deftruction of negroes, by exceffive labour and
" unreafonable punifhments, the furgeon of every
" plantation, by a fubfequent claufe, is required to
" give in, on oath, to the juftices and veftry, an
" annual account of the decreafe and increafe of
" the flaves of fuch plantation, with the caufes of
" fuch decreafe, to the beft of his knowledge,
" judgment, and belief.—On this head the Com-
" mittee cannot but remark, how tender and cau-
" tious

" tious every rational manager muft neceffarily be,
" in the punifhments which he adminifters, who
" confiders that he has a refident infpector into his
" conduct; and that the punifhment of death may
" follow an abufe of his authority."

Here again rifes the fpirit of deception, and holds
up thefe two fpecious, but fallacious claufes, to the
eyes of the people of England at large, who will
not, one in an hundred of them, know that by the
common law, benefit of clergy is allowed, in all
cafes where it is not exprefsly barred by ftatute; and
here we fee that the ftatute does not bar it, therefore the murder of negroes ftood after thefe acts, viz.
acts of 1781 and 1787, juft as it did before, that is
to fay, it was manflaughter, and the punifhment,
touching the hand with a warm iron. This being
the cafe, and the Committee knowing it to be the
cafe when they formed their report, how could they
hold up to the publick fo palpable a deception,
which they could not but know every man in the leaft
verfed in legal difquifitions, would fee through ?—
But the formal and feemingly grave remark that
concludes the laft cited claufe, is intolerable. Beyond a doubt, whatever corrupts the heart, darkens
the underftanding; or how elfe could men of ftrong
abilities fuppofe, that fo palpable a fraud would
pafs undetected, and unexpofed ?

" Neither does the law extend its protection to
" the induftrious and faithful negroe only; provi-
" fion is made for the fupport of fuch fugitives and
" criminals as are apprehended and lodged in the
" gaols and work-houfes of this ifland; the daily
" allowance of good and wholefome food, required
" by

" by Claufe 31ft to be given to every flave in con-
" finement, being abundantly liberal, and, as we
" conceive, unexampled in moft other countries, to
" unhappy perfons in fimilar circumftances."

This is a wife and meritorious claufe. However,
it hath not all the merit that would be attributed to
it by people in England for the following reafons.
Until the paffing of the flave law, of the prefent
feffion, there was no provifion made by law for gaol
deliveries of negroes, in confequence of which,
negroes committed for pretended offences, have
been fuffered to remain in gaol for life, without any
crime proved, without ever being brought to trial
at all, and probably without any offence having been
committed. A man at enmity with his neighbour,
fees that a particular negroe is of the utmoft confequence to his mafter, who, by means of that
negroe, enjoys fome advantage over his neighbours;
perhaps he is an excellent fugar-boiler, a good dif-
tiller, cooper, mafon, fmith, or carpenter; he may
underftand the breaking of horfes, cattle, &c.—or
he rides race-horfes, is a good coachman, butler,—or
fome how or other, he is the caufe of envy to fome
perfon. That man's ox is killed, and he by rewards, or the fear of punifhment, induces one of
his negroes to inform that the envied negroe has
killed it. He is thereupon committed to gaol,
where, no longer exciting envy, he is forgotten, his
mafter dies, or goes off the ifland, and the negroe
remains for years in prifon. Now, in this view, is
there any thing above negative merit, in that legiflature, which omitting to provide for fpeedy trials,
and regular gaol deliveries, does not ftarve the
neglected prifoners to death? Certainly not: but
                                                    fome

some may suppose that no such cases happen — I aver they do: I was present this session, when, amongst other demands brought against the publick by the gaoler of Kingston, two were read and referred to a committee; one for the maintenance of a negroe, who had died in gaol, after having laid there six years, without having been brought to trial; the other, for the maintenance of another negroe, now living, and in gaol, who has been there seven years, without any trial.—The new law has provided for gaol deliveries, at least every three months. Respecting negroes committed, or more properly sent, to the work-house, it must be observed, that whoever pleases may send his own negroes to the work-house, without assigning any reason whatever, and order them to be punished; and is there then much humanity in not starving to death those who are arbitrarily sent to the work-houses, which here are houses of correction, and who are punished not only without trial, but often without crime, and merely at the suggestion of passion or caprice?

" Having thus briefly stated the protection which
" the laws of this island have provided for our slaves,
" in the grand circumstance of personal safety; we
" now proceed to the *second* head, namely, to prove,
" *that the slave-laws in this island are executed with*
" *humanity, mildness, and mercy.*" By the slave-laws
" here alluded to, we understand the laws, and
" clauses of laws, which assign penalties and pu-
" nishments on such offences and transgressions of
" our slaves as affect the publick: and, in order to
" obtain the fullest information on this head, we
" have called on the several clerks of the peace of
" the

" the different precincts and parishes, for returns
" of all trials of slaves, with the charges, convic-
" tion, and punishment severally had thereon, for
" several years last past, viz. From the 1st of Ja-
" nuary 1784, to the 30th of September 1788:
" From these returns we are enabled to state the
" following circumstances :—

" In the parishes and precinct of St. Catherine,
" St. John, St. Dorothy, and St. Thomas in the
" Vale, containing 21,772 slaves, the number of
" capital convictions and executions were four
" only, in the said interval :

" In the parish of St. Andrew, containing 9,613
" slaves, we find only one execution, in the said
" interval :

" In the parishes and precinct of St. Thomas in
" the East, and St. David, containing 23,373 slaves,
" the number of capital convictions and executions
" were ten, in the said interval :

" In the parishes and precinct of St. Mary and
" St. George, containing 22,194 slaves, the num-
" ber of capital convictions and executions were
" four, in the said interval :

" In the parish of St. Ann, containing 13,324
" slaves, the number of capital convictions and
" executions were two, in the said interval :

" In the parish of Trelawny, containing 19,318
" slaves, the number of capital convictions and
" executions were seven, in the said interval :

" In

" In the parifh of St. James, containing 18,546
" flaves, the number of capital convictions and exe-
" cutions were three, in the faid interval :

" In the parifh of Hanover, containing 17,612
" flaves, the number of capital convictions and
" executions were two, in the faid interval :

" In the parifh of Weftmoreland, containing
" 16,700 flaves, the number of capital convictions
" and executions were four, in the faid interval :

" In the parifh of St. Elizabeth, containing.
" 13,280 flaves, the number of capital convictions
" and executions were eight, in the faid interval :

" In the parifhes and precinct of Clarendon and
" Vere, containing 22,234 flaves, the number of
" capital convictions and executions were feven, in
" the faid interval :

" In the feveral towns and parifhes of Kingfton,
" Port-Royal, and Portland, containing 12,928
" flaves, there do not appear to be any capital con-
" victions within the faid period; but the records
" of trials in the town of Kingfton, previous to
" 1787, are not to be found."

" The total appears to be, 52 executions in four
" years and nine months, which is not more than
" 11 per annum for the laft five years, out of
" 210,894 flaves : — a proof of lenity in the exe-
" cution of our criminal laws, not to be furpaffed,
" as we conceive, by any nation in Europe. No-
" thing further, therefore, feems neceffary to be
                                          " added

" added on this head, except the 40th Claufe of
" the prefent Confolidated Slave-Bill, which directs,
" that in all cafes where the punifhment of death
" is inflicted, the execution fhall be performed in a
" publick part of the parifh, and with due folem-
" nity; and care fhall be taken by the gaoler or
" deputy-marfhal, that the criminal is free from
" intoxication at the time of his trial, and from
" thence to, and at, the time of his execution,
" under the penalty of five pounds : and the mode
" of fuch execution is directed to be, hanging by
" the neck, and no other : It is likewife provided,
" that where feveral flaves are capitally convicted
" for the fame offence, one only fhall fuffer death,
" except in cafes of murder or rebellion."

On this part of the Report I fhall be compelled
to renew the charges of fuppreffion of evidence.
To prove that the laws of the ifland afford protection to flaves on the grand article of perfonal fafety,
the Committee ought to have fhewn not only that
the law had affigned adequate penalties and punifhments on white people who abufed, maimed, or
difmembered flaves, but alfo that thofe provifions of
the law had been faithfully exerted for the protection and perfonal fafety of flaves ; neither of which
they have done : for, in the firft cafe, the higheft
punifhment affigned by the laws, at the time the
Report was made, for the moft deliberate and bar-
barous murder of a flave, was applying an iron to
the palm of the murderer's hand, which might be
warm or cold, according to the bribe given to the
executioner ; and this being the extremeft punifhment for aggravated murder, the punifhment for
inferior degrees of cruelty could not be much. I

C   repeat,

repeat, that for difmemberment of flaves, I know
but of one man punifhed, and that fince the people of Britain have interefted themfelves on behalf
of flaves; whereas I know many inftances of difmemberments. I have already hinted at men now
living, who have not only difmembered but murdered fcores of negroes, and yet have never been
called to any account.—On this head, let one inftance
fuffice, which inftance was known to the Committee : A Jew determined to whip one of his negroes
to *death*, and avowed that determination; he began
the lingering murder with his own hands, and
whipped until his ftrength was exhaufted, and then
put the whip into other hands fucceffively, and
urged them on until the tragedy was compleated in
his own prefence, and by his own order : *all which
was proved on his trial,* of *all which he was found*
GUILTY, *convicted, and fentenced*; What ? — Imprifonment for life ? No:—For feven years? No:—
He was fined in all he had ? No :—In what ? FIVE
POUNDS !—with this mockery of God and juftice,
to give it an air of feverity, that he fhould be im-
prifoned until he paid the fine, which he did in-
ftantly, and went out laughing. All this, I fay,
was known to the Committee at the very time the
affertion of the protection afforded to the flaves in
the grand circumftance of perfonal fafety was made.
I deny, that the flave laws have been executed with
humanity, mildnefs, and mercy; and I aver, that
the Committee, at the time they framed this de-
ceptive report, had before them the moft authen-
tick proofs of abominable cruelty in the execution of thofe very laws : they acknowledge that
" *they had callen on the feveral clerks of the peace*
" of the different parifhes, for returns of ALL
" trials

" trials of flaves, with the charges, Convictions,
" and Punishments feverally had thereon," &c.
Now, how comes it, that inftead of All trials,
Convictions, and Punishments had thereon,
the Committee have chofe to report the convictions
of *capital* offences only ? The reafon was this, the
capital convictions were comparatively few in number (which, by the way, fhews the wickednefs of
thofe writers who endeavour to reprefent the negroes as vindictive and irafcible in the extreme)
whereas the difmemberments and other violent
punifhments were fo numerous that they would
not bear infpection, with any hope of impreffing
Britons with the idea which was intended to be
given, that the laws were adminiftered with humanity, mildnefs, and mercy. This was the real
reafon of reporting on the *capital offences only.*

Parifhes and Precinct of St. Thomas and St.
David.—" The number of capital convictions and
" executions were ten." This parifh, neverthelefs, was infamous for difmemberment.

" Parifh of St. Ann's.—Capital convictions and
" executions two." In this parifh, neverthelefs,
there are two men alive at this hour, whofe neighbours fay pofitively, and every one believes, have
each of them murdered fcores of their own negroes, of which murders no inquifition or inquiry
of any kind has been made.

" Parifh of St. James.—Capital convictions and
" executions three." In this parifh one ———,
deftroyed in lefs than three years by cruelty and
abfolute murder 136 of his own negroes, of which

murders

murders no inqueft hath been made or taken ; and yet the Committee fay that the flaves are under the protection of the laws with regard to perfonal fafety.

" In the parifhes of Port-Royal, Portland, and " Kingfton, there do not appear to have been " any capital convictions." How fhould. they appear, when the records by which only they could be fhewn by the clerks of the peace, were not produced ? Had thofe records contained matter favourable to the object of the Committee, they would probably have been found, or rather, they would not have been loft.

" The total appears to be 52 executions, in four " years and nine months." Thefe are the executions by fentence of the law ; had the numbers of private murders been added, there would not have been room to mention lenity.

" On the *third* ground of inquiry, we are to " demonftrate, " *That the laws have made pro-* " *vifion to grant flaves days of reft, and to prevent* " *their being in want of the neceffaries of life."*— " Although we conceive that this affertion has " been fufficiently eftablifhed, by the recital al- " ready given of fuch claufes of our laws as relate " to the fubfiftence of our flaves; yet, as the " words, " fufficient time," in one of the claufes " referred to, left a difcretionary power in the " mafter, we fhall take occafion, in a fubfequent " part of our report, to fhew that the legiflature " has provided a remedy againft any poffible abufe " of fuch difcretionary authority: But the fur- " ther

" ther difcuffion of this fubject is, deferred, until
" we treat of the new flave-bill, paffed the prefent
" feffion."

This article has been obferved on before, and
although it is there fhewn that the provifion, as it
is termed, made by the law, had not had, nor could
be expected to have any operation, yet the committee wifh it to be fuppofed, that the laws amply
provided for the purpofes here mentioned; yet by
referring to the new bill, the committee indirectly
acknowledge the inefficacy of the old laws.

" On the *fourth* and *laft* ground of our re-
" fearches, namely, to demonftrate, " *That the*
" *decreafe of our flaves does not arife from the caufes*
" *affigned in the petitions prefented to the Britifh*
" *Houfe of Commons, but from other caufes not im-*
" *putable to us, and which the people of Great Bri-*
" *tain do not feem to comprehend;*" the Committee,
" after diligent inquiry and inveftigation, are of
" opinion, that the following are the principal
" caufes to which the alleged decreafe of our
" flaves ought juftly to be imputed : 1ft, *The dif-*
" *proportion between the fexes, in the annual im-*
" *portations from Africa:* 2d, *The lofs of new ne-*
" *groes, on or foon after their arrival, from epidemic*
" *difeafes brought from Africa, or contracted in the*
" *voyage.*"

" Does not arife from the caufes affigned," not
folely, but certainly in a very great degree.

" Not imputable to us," this affertion is fo far
juft as it refers to the numbers which perifhed by

C 3   famine

famine for want of the ports being open, and the difproportion between the fexes which is very great, and the difeafes contracted in the voyage; but certainly a great proportion of the decreafe arifes from caufes juftly imputable.

It appears from the Report that 31,181 negroes have perifhed between the report of the fhips and the days of fales; now, if we allow on an average, fifteen days between the days of reports and the days of the fales, and if we allow the paffages from Guinea to the iflands on an average to be four times as long, that is fixty days, and count the mortality on board during all the horrible circumftances of the paffage, to be only in like proportion as to number of deaths, and add thofe numbers to 31,181, the number that perifhed in port, we fhall have the whole number of lives loft by crowding, I may fay, cramming, thofe wretches by hundreds into fhips which are not fufficient to hold properly half the numbers that have been put into them.

Died after their arrivals, — —	31,181
On the paffages, — — —	1,24,724
	1,55,905

One hundred and fifty-five thoufand nine hundred and five negroes perifhed of thofe that have been embarked for Jamaica, fay in port and in paffages. Farther, let us fuppofe, that for all the windward and leeward iflands belonging to Great Britain put together, a number of negroes have been embarked equal to thofe embarked for Jamaica, and that to the French, Spanifh, Dutch, and Danifh iflands and colonies altogether, as many

as

as to the Britifh; and that the mortality has been proportionate to the number, then the account of the lofs of lives will ftand thus:—

Loft of thofe embarked for Jamaica,	-	155905
Ditto, and leeward iflands,	- -	155905
Ditto, foreign colonies, -	- -	311810

623620

Six hundred and twenty-three thoufand fix hundred and twenty! a number at which humanity is petrified with horror. After mature confideration I do folemnly believe the real number to be much nearer the double of this.

The Maroon negroes fhould not be added to the number of negroes now alive in the ifland, in calculating the quantum of increafe of flaves; for thefe people are not the progeny of negroes imported by the Britifh, they are the defcendants of the Spaniards when the ifland was conquered by Penn and Venables, who fled to the mountains and defended their liberty. It is true they have many concubines in the plantations in the lowlands, from which connexions no doubt children have fprung, but as the child follows the condition of the mother, and becomes the flave of the owner of the mother, it is evident thefe children rather incline the balance the other way.

I think the number of free people of colour eftimated at 10,000, is taken much too high.

The

The time of four months allowed after the storms of 1780 and 1781, for the importation of provisions in foreign bottoms, was in reality not more than two months; for, as it was from the States on the continent only that we could expect any quantities of supplies, if we allow one month for the proclamation to reach them, and one month for the passage of the ships, there was not so much as two months for the American merchants to speculate in and collect cargoes of provisions : for undoubtedly towards the latter end of the third month of the proclamation, that is, the second of its promulgation in the states, they would begin to be fearful of their steps in case of contrary winds, or other detention arising after the time limited by the proclamation, and of their being seized. For to add to the calamities of the island, the revenue officers that were about that time sent out from Britain, seemed to be composed of pettyfogging attornies, or of such as had been instructed by them, how to construe the letter of the laws diametrically opposite to the spirit thereof; so that foreigners were terrified from coming into our ports. As to the prolongation for one month, it could hardly answer any good purpose, because by the time that foreigners could receive notice of it, the term of the prolongation would be expired, or expiring, and no time left to bring in this assistance. No man all the while blamed the Lieutenant Governor, because they knew that his hands were tied down by orders from home.

The constitutions of the negroes had been so debilitated and broken down by the former want of wholesome provisions, that they had not strength

to

to fupport themfelves under the return of famine, and dropped off in numbers.

Horrible indeed was the tragedy after the fifth hurricane in 1786; and fo far have the Committee been from exaggerating the calamities of the ifland, by ftating the lofs at 15000 of lives, that I am convinced from much inquiry, that they have ftated *them* too low by feveral thoufands. I cannot be fuppofed to be influenced by refentment from my own loffes on this occafion, for thanks be to the God of mercy, I forefaw and was enabled to provide againft the feveral droughts and confequent famines, fo that I did not lofe the life of a fingle negro, by the want of wholefome provifions: on the contrary, they were more healthy and vigorous than at any other time, fo at leaft other people faid; but I accounted for it from their comparing them with the poor emaciated famine-worn creatures they faw on other plantations, and the contraft was fo ftriking, as could not but claim their attention. This brought about inquiries into my management of my negroes in regard to feeding them; and I have the comfort to be affured, that befide preferving my own negroes, I was the means of fome thoufands more being preferved.

Befide the enormous numbers that perifhed outright during the famine, and which from much inquiry and various relations, I am fully perfuaded exceeded 21,000, I do firmly believe that a far greater number were fo debilitated and broken down in their conftitutions, that they gradually pined and lingered away; but as they died not during the immediate fcarcity, their death was attributed

tributed to fluxes, dropfies, &c. without confidering that thofe difeafes were confequences of the debility induced by the preceding famine. Now, were the whole number of lives loft during the time of actual fcarcity, added to the far greater numbers who fell by its flow effects after the fcarcity was over, though as really deftroyed by the famine as thofe who fell during its rage, the fum would be horrible. But when we confider that had the latter hurricane occurred a few days, ten days fooner, an immenfe quantity of the great corn, the bulk of which was but juft got in when the ftorm commenced, and was the only fpecies of provifion of confequence then in the ifland; I fay, that had that hurricane occurred ten days or a fortnight fooner, that would have, great part of it, been deftroyed: the certain confequences of which would have been univerfal famine, for every inferior fpecies of provifion had been before exhaufted. The ifland muft inevitably have been depopulated. Unthinking minds fay, that the deftruction that did occur, and the general deftruction which by divine mercy we barely efcaped, had it alfo come upon us, were the effects of thofe tempefts and droughts and famines, and the inevitable works of God: the tempefts, droughts, and confequent famines were fo no doubt, and wrought for wife, good, and ultimately gracious purpofes; but if the deftruction of fo many poor flaves are to be attributed to Providence, it muft not be to its operations on the elements, fo much as by the blindnefs which was fuffered to come over the underftandings of thofe in the charge of government, to fuch a degree as to tie down the Governor of a colony at the diftance of 5000 miles,

fo

fo as that not only the property and happinefs of that colony, but even its exiftence fhould be hazarded, rather than that he fhould depart from the regulations made in Britain. What will pofterity think of fuch monftrous abufe of the powers entrufted in the hands of government for the benefit, protection, and general good of thofe who gave thofe powers into their hands? Nay, what will they think of a people who would fubmit to fee daily facrifices to the fpirit of obftinacy, which a few men on the other fide of the globe called wifdom? There was an eafy remedy for thofe terrible evils, and which, if it had been timeoufly applied, would have faved the lives of (in my opinion) more than 30,000 people; but we muft believe that the fpirit of blindnefs had ftricken the minds of the people alfo, as well as thofe of their princes and rulers.

The Committee ftate two principal caufes in addition to thofe mentioned before of the decreafe of the negroes. 1ft, The great proportion of deaths that happen among the negroes newly imported; and, 2d, the lofs amongft the negro infants.

With refpect to the firft, great part of thofe deaths are the effects of the fame caufes which occafion fo many deaths during the paffage from Africa, and in the ports of the iflands where they arrive, and before they are landed; thefe are perturbation of mind, foul and putrid air, water, and provifions, forrow for what they have left, and dread of what they are going to.

For

For observations on the second, see the notes on the examinations of Messrs. Chisholme, Anderson, and Quier, annexed to the Report.

I have no doubt, but that the regulations made by the British Act of Parliament, in restraining and proportioning the number of negroes to be taken on board to the tonnage of the ships, especially if farther regulations should be added, respecting the time beyond which ships shall not remain on the coast of Africa, quantity of water, &c. will be the means not only of preserving the lives of thousands on the passage, but of many more, by preventing the infectious putrid disorders, which contaminate the blood of those who do not immediately sink under it.

" The offender will have the security, both of " a grand and petit jury."

This was struck out of the bill by the Council, and as the law now stands, there is no grand jury, and the petit jury consists but of nine. The assembly were obliged to concur; as they found after a conference of the two Houses, which lasted two days, the bill would be lost if they did not acquiesce in the alteration; nor indeed would it have passed at all, but for the alarm that was caught on the arrival, I may say the providential arrival, of a packet from Britain, which brought no dispatches but for the governor, and naval commanders in chief, and the Governor's declarations that the said packet was sent out by government expressly on the negroe business. This alarmed the Council, and such of the House of Assembly as had opposed
the

the moft beneficial regulations in the bill. Which
bill, as now paffed into a law, after all the alter-
ations by the council, ftill is an immenfe melioration of the fituation of the negroes, if faithfully
executed, amongft which this article is the firft;
that of providing gaol deliveries every three months
at leaft, by PUBLICK TRIALS, not by dark and
packed juntos in a corner; by the Juftices being
compelled to grant warrants on any information to
bring before them negroes difmembered, mutilated,
or cruelly treated—this laft is, I believe, not in the
bill exprefsly, but I hope Juftices will think it
implied;— by appointing councils of protection for
the abufed flave, without which an attempt to obtain redrefs would have been deemed an unpardon-
able crime, and punifhed with ftill greater cruelty;—
by the providing provifion for, and in fome cafes
declaring them free;—by obliging the proprietors
of flaves or other reprefentatives to give in on oath,
accounts annually of the increafe or decreafe of
their flaves, and the refpective Doctors who attend
the plantations, to certify on oath the caufe of the
deaths;—by giving in like manner accounts of the
quantity of cloathing fupplied the negroes, and the
quantity of ground cultivated in provifions, and
the time allowed the flaves to cultivate their own
grounds: all thefe are capital regulations, and if
faithfully adhered to, will be attended with the
happieft effects. Good laws can do much, but it
is from the manners of a people that they muft
derive their beft effects.

" Neither courts of quarter feffion nor juftices,
" fhall have power to order any flave to be muti-
" lated or maimed for any offence whatever."

What

What muſt have been the practice that made it requiſite to reſtrain courts and magiſtrates from maiming and mutilating?

The clauſe reſpecting the converſion and baptiſm of ſlaves is duſt for the eyes of the people in Britain. It puts me in mind of a circumſtance that occurred on board a coaſting veſſel, which was blown off the coaſt, the maſter and mate of which were totally ignorant of the methods of keeping an account of the ſhip's way in the ocean, and of aſcertaining her place and ſituation to the land; which the ſeamen obſerving were greatly alarmed at. " I wiſh," ſaid the maſter to the mate, " our " poor wives knew where we are:"—" I wiſh," ſaid one of the ſeamen, " we knew ourſelves where " we are." I apprehend there is ſomething requiſite previous to *maſters*, *miſtreſſes*, and *overſeers* endeavouring to inſtruct their negroes in the principles of the *Chriſtian religion*.

" Another very important object of this bill is " the correction of two material errors which had " been accidentally made in the conſolidated ſlave " bill of laſt year: The words, " *without benefit* " *of clergy*," in the clauſe which aſſigns the pu " niſhment of death to perſons wantonly killing " a negro or other ſlave, having been undeſign " edly omitted—theſe are now reſtored:—And " another clauſe in the ſaid conſolidated ſlavebill, " which inflicted puniſhments on perſons wanton ". ly and cruelly beating ſlaves, and impriſoning " them without ſufficient ſupport, having been " interpreted not to extend to ſuch ſlaves as were " the

" the property of the offender, has been amended,
" and the protection which it affords is now ex-
" tended to all flaves, without diftinction."

How does this comport with the grave obfervations and cautions cited in pages, 6, 7 and 8.

" Further, in the view of reftraining arbi-
" tary punifhments, it is, by the faid bill, enact-
" ed, That no flave on any plantation or fettle-
" ment, or in any of the workhoufes or gaols in
" this ifland, fhall receive more than ten lafhes at
" a time, and for one offence, unlefs the owner,
" attorney, guardian, executor, adminiftrator, or
" overfeer of fuch plantation or fettlement, or fu-
" pervifor of fuch workhoufe, or keeper of fuch
" gaol, fhall be prefent; and no fuch owner, at-
" torney, guardian, executor, adminiftrator, or
" overfeer, fupervifor, or gaol-keeper, fhall, on
" any account, punifh a flave with more than
" thirty-nine lafhes, at one time, and for one of-
" fence, under the penalty of five pounds for
" each offence, to be recovered againft the perfon
" directing or permitting fuch punifhment.

I do not like the manner in which this claufe is
expreffed, I fear it will be greatly abufed, " at one
" time AND for one offence," I think it fhould
have been, *for one offence:* as it now ftands, I apprehend the number of lafhes limited by the law
will not prevent the repetition of the fame number
of lafhes, the day after the firft whipping is inflicted, and fo *de die in diem,* to the extent of the
rage and cruelty of the perfon who directs the punifhment.

" Another

" Another object of this bill (as hath been al-
" ready obferved) is to fecure to our flaves days
" of reft, and fufficient time to cultivate their
" grounds, in order to prevent their being in want
" of the neceffaries of life : For which purpofe,
" after reciting, that although it hath been cuf-
" tomary with the planters in this ifland to allow
" their flaves one day in every fortnight (exclu-
" five of Sundays) ; yet this indulgence not being
" compulfory, it is enacted by the faid bill,
" that the flaves belonging to, or employed on,
" every plantation or fettlement, fhall, over and
" above the ufual holidays allowed them at
" Chriftmas, Eafter, and Whitfuntide, be allow-
" ed one day in every fortnight, to cultivate their
" own provifion-grounds (exclufive of Sundays),
" except during the time of crop, under the pe-
" nalty of ten pounds, to be recovered againft the
" overfeer, or other perfon having the care of fuch
" flaves."

With comparatively very few indeed was it cuftomary, and what follows, " yet not being com-
" pulfory," proves what I have afferted in a former
note.
" Laftly, with intention to prevent, as far as
" poffible, the great mortality which has been
" ftated to prevail among the new-born negro in-
" fants, it is alfo enacted, That, in cafe it fhall
" appear to the fatisfaction of the juftices and
" veftry of each parifh, from the returns re-
" quired to be made annually, there has been a
" natural increafe in the number of flaves on any
" fuch plantation, pen, or other fettlement, the
" overfeer fhall be entitled to receive from the
" owner

" owner or proprietor of fuch plantation, pen, or
" other fettlement, the fum of twenty fhillings
" for every flave born on fuch plantation, pen, or
" other fettlement, and which fhall be then living,
" at the time of giving in fuch annual returns;
" and the owner or proprietor of fuch plantation,
" pen, or other fettlement, fhall have a deduction,
" from the firft of his or her publick taxes that
" fhall become due, of the fum fo paid to the
" overfeer, on producing a certificate of the jufti-
" ces and veftry of fuch increafe, and a receipt
" of the overfeer for the fum fo paid."

This is a wife regulation, and more good may
be expected from it than what would arife from the
pecuniary reward. It will, I hope, and believe, be
the means of introducing a laudable ambition
amongft the overfeers to take care of the negroes;
and indeed I think that from the infamy that will
in a little time ftigmatize fuch neglect, or at
leaft abufe, of them, much may be expected; but
ftill more might be reafonably expected were the
flave trade totally abolifhed now, or after the importation of more females.

The Committee proceed to fay, that " the mea-
" fure of abolifhing the African flave trade muft
" ruin the fugar iflands."

I know a plantation in St. Ann's, which in 17
years hath by procreation, and without purchafe,
doubled its number of negroes, and two over. I
know an inftance where a deed of gift was made
of eight negroes in the year 1744, of the progeny of which eight negroes, there are now in

D   1788,

1788, above fixty-four, that is juft octuple, the original ftock in forty-four years. The negroes on my own plantation, which within the laft feven years has had its labour nearly doubled, by having many maffy buildings to erect, and almoft the whole grounds to fence by ftone walls, and many other extraordinary things to do, keep up their numbers, and increafe, notwithftanding the peculiar difadvantages arifing from thofe circumftances, from the repeated hurricanes and their confequences in that period, and above all, notwithftanding that there is a great difproportion of the females to the males, of which former we at this time are deficient forty-three. Had I attended to the circumftance of proportioning the fexes when I firft came into poffeffion of the eftate, I am convinced that by this time it would have over-flowed with negroes, as would every plantation where the number of the fexes are duly propor-tioned, and humanity is exercifed. This being my decided opinion, I am under no felfifh appre-henfion from the abolition of the flave trade, nor need any one elfe be fo, who will act agreeably to the dictates of confcience and common fenfe.

Yet it muft be acknowledged, and I acknow-ledge it without reluctance, that the difpropor-tion between the fexes is the fource of infinite mifery. It is the grand caufe of the general profti-tution of the negroe women, of difeafe, quarrel, bloodfhed, incontinence, and want of population.*

NOTES

* It were to be wifhed our Author had been more explicit on this interefting point, the difproportion of the fexes. He feems to have formed his opinion from the particular fituation of his own eftate, rather

NOTES on the examination of JAMES CHISHOLME, Efq. annexed to the Report.

" During fourteen years he has had the care
" of four thoufand negroes"—what fort of medical
care

rather than upon a general examination into the matter.   The evils
he here mentions arife not from the difproportion of the fexes, but
from their *unequal diftribution*.   There are at this time 480,000
negro flaves in all the Britifh fugar colonies.   The *Africans* (who
are imported in the proportion * of three females to five males)
cannot exceed one-fifth of the whole, or 96,000; for thefe all die
off in 15 years; and one-third in the firft three years.   But about
13 years ago, the war put a ftop to their importation; fo
that four-fifths of all purchafed before that time muft be dead, and,
fince the peace in 1783, only 85,000 have been imported and kept
in the Britifh iflands, and even of thefe a great part is now dead.
Among the creoles or native flaves, who form four-fifths of the
whole, or 384,000, the proportion of the fexes follows the courfe
of nature.

Thus the negro flaves in all the Britifh fugar iflands divide themfelves into   Females   Males
   384·000 creoles   —   192·000   192·000
   96·000 imported Africans (3 to 5) 36·000   60.000

   480·000   Females, 228·000—Males, 252·000
or exactly *nineteen* females to *twenty-one* males—a proportion not
very different from that of the births of the fexes throughout the
world, viz. of 19 females to 20 males.†

 But the able calculator juft referred to hath amply proved, that
though the fexes *be born* in this laft proportion, yet the number of
females actually living, at any one time, is greater than that of the
males.‡   Among many inftances to prove this, he adduces the following remarkable ones.   That temperate and healthy clafs of men,
the church minifters, and profeffors of the Univerfities in Scotland,
have a fund for the maintenance of their widows.   The annual

---

* Jamaica Report.
† Price on Rev. pay. p. 16.
‡ Id. vol. I. p. 8, 81, 126, 366, 373, and vol. II. p. 8, 145, 245.

medium

care one man can give to four thoufand negroes, every two hundred of which on an average are on plantations

medium of their weddings is 30, and the annual medium of widows who have come upon the fund, for 35 years, is 19 and 1-10th. Of the 30 annual marriages then 19 and 1-10th are diffolved by the death of hufbands, and not 11 by the death of wives; confequently the number of widows actually living is to the number of widowers as 19 and 1-10th is to 10 and 9-10ths, or nearly double.—In nine years ending in 1763, there were living in the whole kingdom of Sweden 10 females to 9 males. At Edinburgh, in 1743, there were found 4 females to 3 males.

But, what is more to our purpofe, according to Montefquieu more girls than boys are born in hot climates.* And the accurate Kempfer † relates, that at Meaco there were found, by actual enumeration, 223.573 females, and only 182.072 males. Thus every circumftance confpires to prove that there are more females than males living in the world (efpecially in hot climates); and there is not the fhadow of a reafon to fuppofe that the creole negroes are an exception to what appears to be the general order of procedure.

In all countries men live more irregularly, and are more liable to accidents than women, and every caufe unfavourable to human life operates with peculiar force on negro men. They diffipate their vigour on a plurality of wives. It is well known that, to vifit them (when their wives happen to be removed to a diftance) the hufbands make very long nocturnal excurfions; returning to their drudgery the next morning, fatigued and difpirited. They are more refractory than the women; they oftener run away, and ftay longer out. On the whole they commit more faults, and confequently fuffer more inhuman treatment.—Thefe are among the caufes which contribute to render the lives of men flaves fhorter than thofe of women flaves. The Guinea traders acknowledge that the men muft be confined in chains, and the Jamaica Report complain of the diforders arifing from it, which carry off great numbers in feafoning. The deaths in feafoning muft be therefore principally among the men, and probably leave the fexes of the feafoned Africans nearly in an equal proportion. In the ifland of Nevis, female flaves are to the males as five to four. This is an old fettled ifland, and confifts chiefly of creoles.

The inconveniences and evils therefore, which our author complains of do not arife from the *inequality*, but from the *unequal diftribu-*

* Efp. de Loix, liv. 16. ch. 4.   † Id. ibid.

tion

plantations remote from each other, and this be-
fides his practice amongft the white people, let the
impartial judge.

" That a great proportion of negro infants perifh
" between the fifth and fourteenth days after their
" birth; he believes nearly one-fourth part of all
" that are born."

I believe on moft plantations this may be the
cafe, but I am confident it will not be fo long:
for, formidable as thefe medical men may affect to
reprefent the diforder, the effects of which are fo
fatal, it is by no means impoffible to prevent it;
and I affert this on my own experience, for on my
plantations this diforder was as frequent as on
others, until I came to infpect and refide on them
myfelf, fince which it is become as rare as it was
common before.

The account Mr. Chifholme gives of the diforder, in my opinion, points out the cure. If the
diforder arifes from irritation of the nerves of the
umbilicus, how eafy to prevent it? Prevent the
caufe, and you prevent the effect.

tion of the fexes. Weft India property is in a ftate of perpetual fluctu-
ation. When eftates are broken up, thofe who, like our Author, have
the command of money buy the males (whether creoles or Africans)
leaving the females to be purchafed by poorer men. Hence, on
fome eftates, the males predominate, and on others, the females.
The total difregard paid in fuch cafes, to the feelings and connec-
tions of negroes as human creatures, and even as animals, gives
rife to all the mifery our Author deplores; independent of the inequality of the fexes, which we have proved has in reality no
exiftence.

EDITOR.

" That

" That if he is right in his theory, refpecting
" the caufe of this complaint, it will be fuppofed
" that the remedy is obvious, as it will be only
" directing a greater attention to be paid to the
" dreffing and cleanlinefs of the infant during the
" period above alluded to: But, fimple as this may
" appear in theory, thofe who are much converfant
" with negroes, will be aware of the difficulty, if
" not impoffibility, of putting it in practice, in
" a degree fufficient to anfwer the purpofe : For,
" fuch is the ignorance, obftinacy, and inatten-
" tion of the negroes; fo little regard have they
" for each other, and fo averfe are they to exe-
" cuting the directions of white people, when re-
" pugnant to their own prejudices, that he believes
" the evil can never be wholly remedied, while
" we are obliged to employ negroes as nurfes."

Here we fee that the gentleman was perfectly
aware of what he conceives would prevent this
deftructive diforder, which he himfelf fays carries off
nearly one of every four of all the negro children
born in the ifland. Let the humane, let the ftatef-
man confider and reflect on the continual exiftence
of a caufe that annually diminifhes one-fourth of
the people. We fee that Mr. Chifholme attributes
the caufe of this diforder not being prevented to the
ignorance, obftinacy, and inattention of negroes.
Will not the fenfible reader of his anfwers conceive,
that before we admit the negligence and inattention of a mother to her infant to be the caufe of its
deftruction, there would be more juftice and probability in confidering that fome part of the caufe
at leaft arifes from medical men, who, by taking
charge of fuch numbers of negroes, have not time

to

to inftruct them, and diffipate that ignorance (the caufe of obftinacy) which is attended with fuch fatal effects ?

" That a very great number of newly-imported
" negroes are loft by difeafes, the predifpofing
" caufes of which they bring to this country along
" with them : Moft new negroes, when firft land-
" ed, are much fubject to putrid complaints, arifing
" from a fcorbutic habit contracted during the
" voyage, which frequently manifefts itfelf foon
" after they are landed, in putrid dyfenteries, or
" by foul ulcers, tending ftrongly to mortifica-
" tion. Many negroes, while aboard, are affected
" with the moft virulent venereal complaints;
" others have the yaws; fome, malignant ulcers;
" all of which, when the day of fale draws near,
" are, by the management of the fhip's furgeon,
" dried up, and the morbid matter repelled into
" the fyftem, fo that the furface of the fkin fhall
" appear clean and fmooth for a time, but which
" afterwards creates the moft dreadful complaints,
" too frequently baffling all attempts to cure.

The putrid complaints arife from putrid air, putrid water, and uncleanlinefs occafioned almoft altogether by the too great numbers crammed into comparatively fmall fhips in a torrid climate—want of good water and provifions, and ventilators, to purify the air.

NOTES

NOTES on the Examination of ADAM ANDER-
SON, Practitioner in Physick and Surgery.

" That with one partner he had the physical care
" of near 4000 slaves"—by *physical care* is meant,
that he and his partner were the physicians, surgeons, apothecaries, and men midwives to 4000.

" That one-fourth of negroe infants perish of
" the tetanus, and but one-tenth of the white in-
" fants,"—the cause is obvious; forty times the
care is taken of the whites, and the consequence
of that care is the difference in the proportion of
deaths.

To the irritation of the umbilicus, assigned as
the cause of the tetanus by Doctor Chisholme,
this gentleman adds that of the putrid matter
suffered to generate during (and he might have said,
and after) the separation of that cord, both which,
with the fatal consequences, I shall by and by
shew are most easily prevented.

" That he does not believe the disorder, in
" general, is owing to any improper mode of
" treatment of the infant, as he has often known
" it occur, notwithstanding the greatest care ; and
" that, from the rapidity of the disorder, and the
" tender age of the patient, he knows of no cer-
" tain remedy that succeeded, either from the ap-
" plication of opiates, or any other medicine, once
" in twenty times : That it occurs in high and
" healthy situations as well as in low ones, in
" mountainous districts, as well as those near the
" sea side."

In

In all thefe circumftances I differ totally from the doctor.

" That he is of opinion, that many negroe
" children die of that diforder peculiar to the
" Africans, called the yaws, particularly if they
" are infected during the firft year; which the
" mothers in general attempt to effect, on purpofe
" to excufe themfelves from labour."

" Who fhall decide when doctors difagree?" Some doctors are of the fame opinion refpecting the fmall pox.—And I, who am no doctor, but who in the courfe of my peregrinations have frequently been obliged to fupply, as well as I could, the place of doctor, furgeon, and apothecary, both to myfelf and hundreds of others, and through mercy with no fmall fuccefs—I fay, I differ wholly from the doctor in this point, and think that at no time can a negroe have the yaws with fuch probability of get-ing eafily through them, as when nourifhed from his mother's breaft.

" That he is of opinion, notwithftanding thofe
" inconveniencies already enumerated, there is very
" confiderable increafe of negroes on the properties
" of this ifland, particularly in the parifh where he
" refides."

Viz. the parifh of Saint Ann's.—It is in this parifh where the inftance, quoted in a former note of the negroes on a plantation having doubled and more in feventeen years, occurred. But it is alfo in this parifh where the inftance is of one man having buried in a few years 300 and odd negroes.
The

The fact is, that every parish in the ifland is generally healthy, and all of them unhealthy in fome
particular fituations; but the great caufes of increafe or decreafe is not the parifh, but the particular regimen and management on particular plantations.

" That the loffes fuftained in feafoning newly-
" imported negroes, are chiefly owing to the many
" diforders they bring with them, either from
" Africa, or contracted on board fhip; fuch as,
" venereals, the yaws, and old habitual ulcers."

" The number of obftinate cafes he has met
" with, induced him to inquire of furgeons that
" had been in that trade, refpecting the mode of
" treatment during the voyage; and that he has
" been informed, it was cuftomary to fupprefs ve-
" nereals by aftringent injections; to caufe the
" yaws and ulcers to difappear by ifchuretic wafhes;
" and on the day of fale, or a few days before, to
" hide the fcars with blacking and palm-oil: That
" the epidemic dyfentery is frequent on board
" fhip; and though the furgeons have a method
" of concealing it on the day of fale, in fome mea-
" fure, by aftringents, yet it frequently breaks out
" after the negroes have landed, with double fury:
" Of which he remembers the following re-
" markable inftance in Colin Campbell, of Saint
" Ann's, having bought thirty negroes in King-
" fton; an epidemic dyfentery broke out among
" them foon after their arrival at the plantation, of
" which twenty-four of them died; the diforder
" was communicated to the reft of the negroes on
" the

" the plantation, and several of them likewise fell
" a sacrifice to it."

This gentleman agrees with the others in the un-
doubted fact, that negroes bring here with them
putrid diseases, contracted on board the ships during
the voyage.—All which testimonies it is to be
hoped will induce the British legislature, whose
right it is to regulate, direct, and controul the
general Commerce of the Empire, to attend to and
provide the necessary remedies against these very per-
nicious and ruinous effects of putridity.

NOTES on the EXAMINATION of
JOHN QUIER.

This gentleman also hath had for the greater
part of twenty-one years the care of 4000 to 5000
negroes. I shall here observe, that to a regiment
of five or six hundred men there is one surgeon,
who hath one or more mates or assistants; that to
each ship of war, having on board from three to
five hundred men, there is also a surgeon and surgeon's mates. Now if a surgeon and surgeon's
mates are necessary to five hundred men, all col-
lected in a small space, what care can one or two
men, acting as physicians, surgeons, apothecaries,
and occasionally men midwives—I say, what care
can they take of 4000 or 5000 negroes, every
two hundred of whom, on an average, are on a
plantation distant some miles from the other, be-
sides his or their practice amongst the white fami-
lies, each of which is also distant from the others?
I ap-

I apprehend it will be thought much eafier, under fuch circumftances, to find fault with the ignorance, obftinacy, and inattention of fuch negroes, than to take care of them, inform, perfuade, or watch over them for good. Once, twice, or thrice in a week, to gallop to a plantation, to take a peep into the hofpital, or hot-houfe, as it is called, write in a book, " bleed this," " purge that," " blifter another," " here give an opiate," " there the bark," is not, in my opinion, taking care of, though it may be called taking charge of, the healths of 4000 or 5000 negroes.

But to proceed with Doctor Quier's examination. We fhall fee that he attributes the diforders to which the negroe children are incident, to the want of cleanlinefs; the obftinate attachment of negroe women to their own old cuftoms; and particularly to their not fhifting the child's cloaths, fometimes from want of linen, and other neceffaries, proper for new-born infants. It is eafy, and perhaps convenient, to throw blame on negroe women, but here the truth comes out at laft, and the word *fometimes*, muft be confidered as a defenfive falvo, which each plantation under the doctor's care will apply to the others, and none to themfelves; and which if the doctor had not put in, it is probable the 5000 or 5000 negroes, of which he tells us he has the care, would have prefently been reduced to 400 or 500.

" That the negroe women, whether flaves or
" free, do not, in his opinion, breed fo fre-
" quently, as the women amongft the labouring
" poor in Great Britain: that he afcribes this
　　　　　　　　　　　　　　　　" chiefly

" chiefly to the promifcuous intercourfe, which
" the greater number of negroe women indulge
" themfelves in with the other fex. That he be-
" lieves the abortions, which he thinks to be ra-
" ther frequent amongft them, to be afcribable to
" the fame caufe : That he has not met with any
" cafes of abortion, which he could fairly impute
" to ill ufage or exceffive labour : That moderate
" labour is beneficial to pregnant women, as being
" the beft means of preferving general health."

I am afraid the reafon here affigned, by the doctor,
for many of the abortions, is but too true; it is
the natural confequence of the difproportion in the
number of the fexes. But when the doctor fays he
has not met with any cafes of abortion which he
could "fairly impute to ill ufage or exceffive labour:"
pleafe to recollect what I have faid above on the ex-
preffion *fometimes*, which, I apprehend, means
much the fame; and I wifh the doctor could, with
fafety to his practice, have ufed the fame word,
inftead of *not* and *any*; at leaft, if this alteration of
words be not an amendment, I will fay the doctor
is fingularly happy in his fituation.

" That the cuftom of carrying young children
" into the field, in the manner, and with the pre-
" cautions it is now practifed, is by no means hurt-
" ful to the infants."

I am of opinion, generally fpeaking, that the
more both infants and adults are in the open air
the better; but the doctor muft allow me to diffent
from his affertion in fome particular cafes; and let
others judge. Suppofe an infant tied on its
mother's

mother's back, and carried to the field, then laid in a bowl or tray, expofed to the direct rays of the fun; fhould a fudden and heavy rain fall, as is very common in thefe climates, I fay, *that* can hardly be beneficial to the infant, and ftill lefs fo its remaining in wet rags. I mention this for two reafons, one is, to fhew that thofe medical gentlemen have fuppreffed whatever might tend to give an unfavourable idea of our lenity to the negroes; and the other is to fhew how neceffary it is to have fome means of fhelter for the negroes, either by erecting tents, or building fheds contiguous to the fields, in heavy, though tranfient fhowers, and to call them from the fields when it appears that the rain will continue. I am led to this laft obfervation by having been an eye-witnefs, when I was laft at ——: Upwards of forty negroes were kept at work in the open field for more than four hours, that is, till night fhut in, during a conftant and heavy rain.

I am obliged to conclude abruptly, but may add fomething more on this fubject by another conveyance.

I am,

Yours, &c.

* * *

F I N I S.